THIS BOOK IS FOR

W9-BKB-372

WOO HOO!
YOU'RE DOING GREAT!

WOO HOO
DOING

TO ANNIE!

Little, Brown and Company
Hachette Book Group, 1290 Avenue of the Americas, New York, NY 10104
The Little, Brown name and logo are trademarks of Hachette Book Group, Inc.
ISBN: 978-0-316-48679-8   PRINTED IN CHINA   APS   10 9 8 7 6 5 4 3 2 1   First Edition: March 2023

YOU'RE GREAT!

by Sandra Boynton

LB
Little, Brown and Company
New York Boston

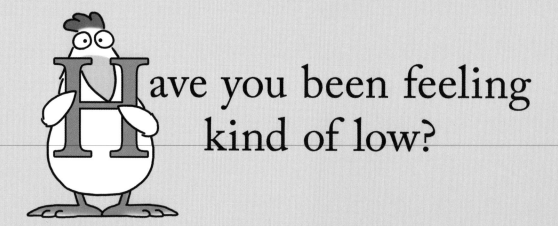

Have you been feeling
kind of low?

A little lost? A little slow?

Perhaps unsure of what to do?

And how to do it?

Is that you?

Or are you feeling
quite upended?

Or is it **ALL** too much for you?
So much to learn.
So much to do.

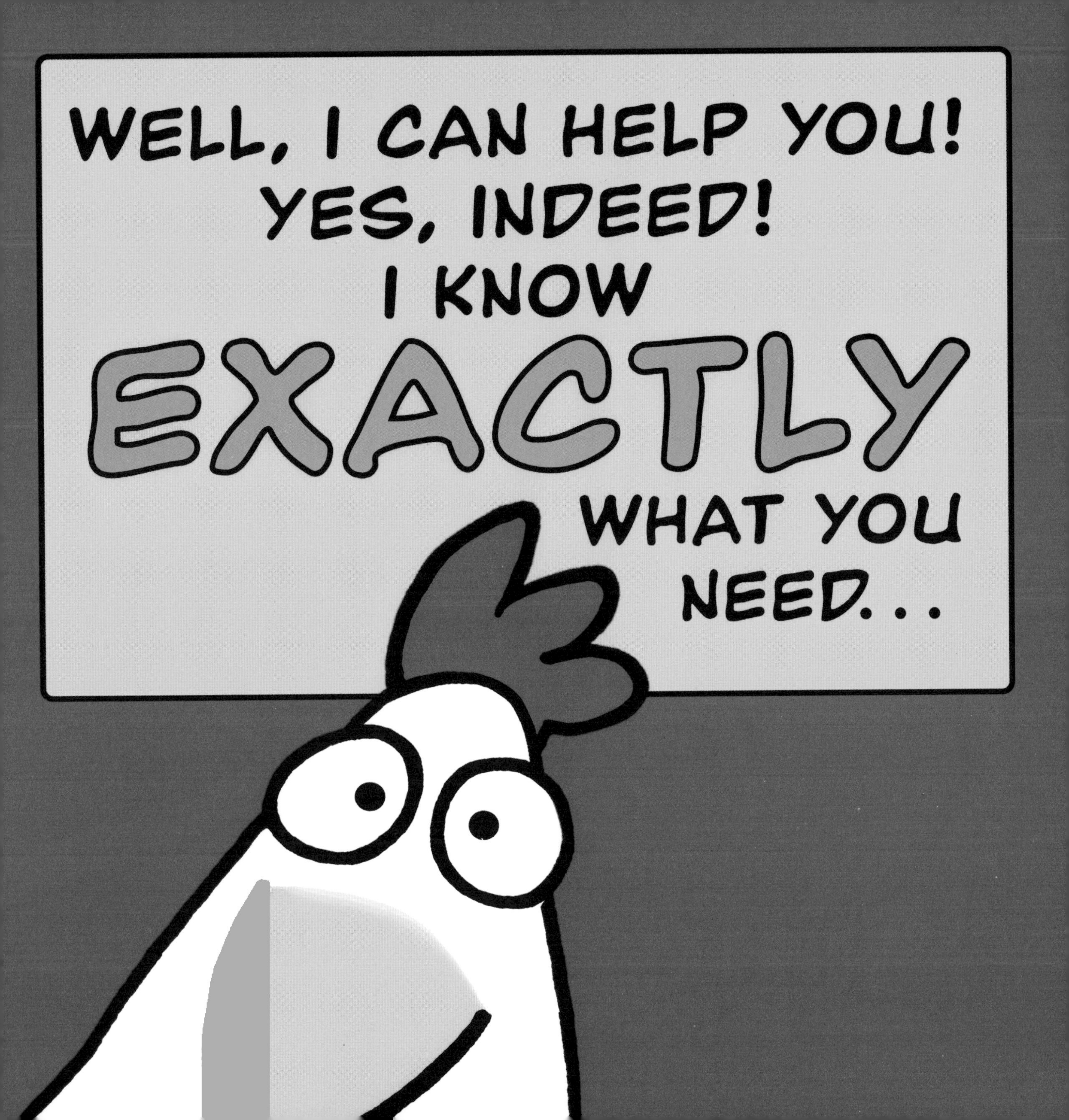
WELL, I CAN HELP YOU!
YES, INDEED!
I KNOW
EXACTLY
WHAT YOU
NEED...

TO WAVE AND CHEER!

HOO!

AND YOU'RE IN LUCK!
I'M HERE!
RIGHT HERE!

THERE'S SURELY NOTHING MORE FANTASTIC THAN SOMEONE WHO'S ENTHUSIASTIC!

Are you learning how to skate?

Are you practicing
ballet?

WOO HOO!
YOU'RE
A-OKAY!

Did you teach yourself

to bake?

WOO HOO! YOU MADE THAT CAKE!

WOO HOO! WAY TO TAP!

ME. UP.

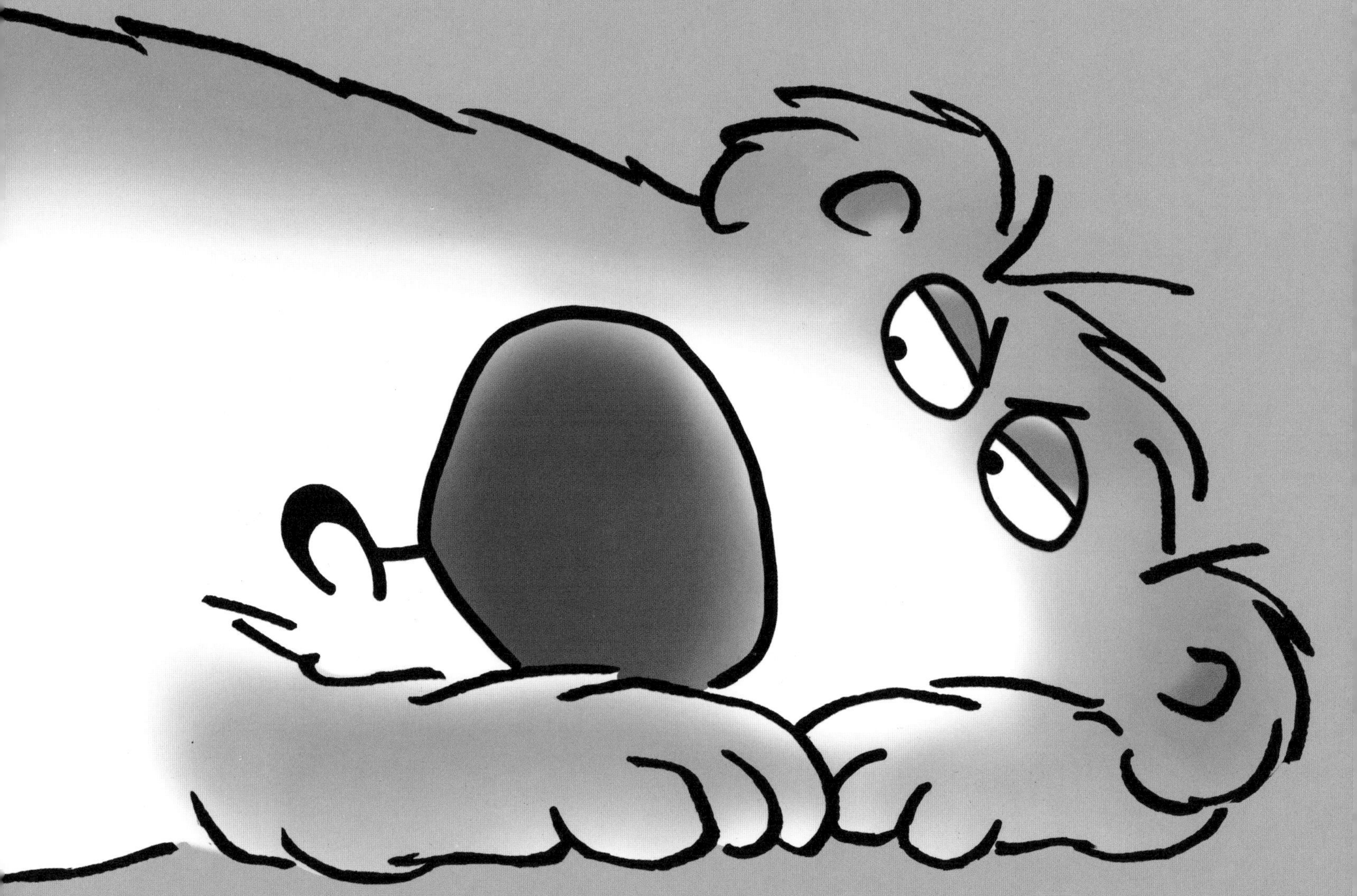

It's often very nice to hear an encouraging word, a kindly cheer.

And it helps to say a big **WOO HOO** to someone who is feeling blue.

But I think perhaps the best
WOO HOO...

...is the one
you say
each day
to you.